Jumping Horse Press
Philadelphia, PA
www.jumpinghorsepress.com

ISBN 978-0-615-55671-0

Harry
The Carousel Horse

For Ned and Maggie

May you always dream!

Karin

Dedicated to horse lovers everywhere

Harry
The Carousel Horse

Written by Karin Tetlow   Illustrated by Tessa Guze

Harry was a white horse who lived on the carousel at the Mall. He was not happy. None of the children wanted to ride him.

The children chose the other horses. Becky always rode Blue, her favorite blue horse. Kirk preferred Red, his favorite red horse.

Blue and Red talked to Harry and tried to cheer him up. But all Harry could say was "It's not fair. It's not fair. I want the children to ride me, not you!"

His mouth turned down and he looked very disagreeable and grouchy.

Harry was still grouchy that night when all the horses nibbled grass on the Mall. He turned his back on Blue and Red and sulked.

Bill, the man in charge of the horses, put his hand on Harry.
"I have a suggestion for you Harry. Tonight, before you go to
sleep, ask for a dream. Say 'Please help me. I want the
children to ride me. Tell me what I should do."

That night Harry had a dream.

In the dream, he first visited the magnificent Gold Horse. Looking up at him he asked, "Magnificent Gold horse, why do you have a rider and I don't?"

The Gold Horse looked down on Harry and answered, "I carry a saint who was a famous warrior. She chose me to ride into battle. Now I carry her for ever."

Harry backed away. "I don't want to go into battle. I'd be afraid," he said.

Next he visited Horsey, a rocking horse who belonged to Isaac. "Horsey, you have Isaac who rides you. I don't have anybody to ride me. Why?"

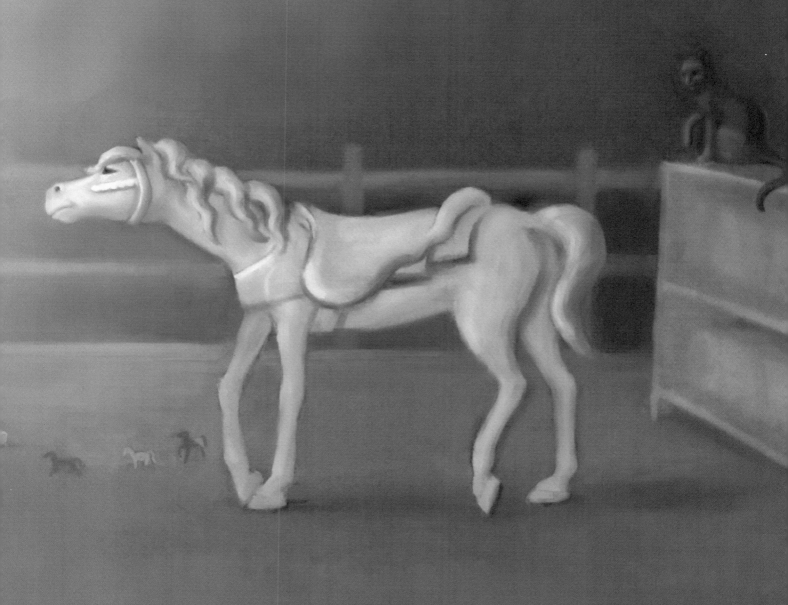

"I don't know about you," said Horsey. "All I know is that Isaac loves me and rides me all the time. He shouts Go, Go and we gallop very fast."

Still not getting an answer to his question, Harry continued dreaming and met Violet. Violet had beautiful violet eyes and lived on a farm.

"Violet, you have many children ride you. Why don't they want to ride me?" asked Harry.

"I have to be very patient and walk slowly," answered Violet. "My riders have disabilities and cannot balance very well. They need an adult to walk beside us. I love carrying them because they are happy sitting on me."

Harry admired Violet for helping people. But he suspected he was not patient enough to walk slowly. To his surprise he felt a little smile on his face. So he smiled a little smile at Violet and dreamed on.

This time he flew for hundreds of miles over towns and play-
grounds and beaches and a very large, wide, ocean until he
came to a round green hill.

There he met Will, another white horse. Will was very old. He had no rider.

Harry spoke to him. "Will, you have no rider. That is so unfair!" Will lifted his head and said, "Many people want to ride me. But I am content as I am. I don't want a rider."

Harry could not understand this. "But all horses have riders except you and me. I want lots of people to ride me! Why don't you want a rider?"

Will answered, "I used to want riders because I was lonely. When nobody wanted to sit on my back, I cried and then I got very grouchy and disagreeable."

"I get grouchy and disagreeable too!" said Harry. "I turn my back on my friends Blue and Red."

Will listened sympathetically and said, "One day I was tired of being grouchy and disagreeable. I asked myself what makes me happy?"

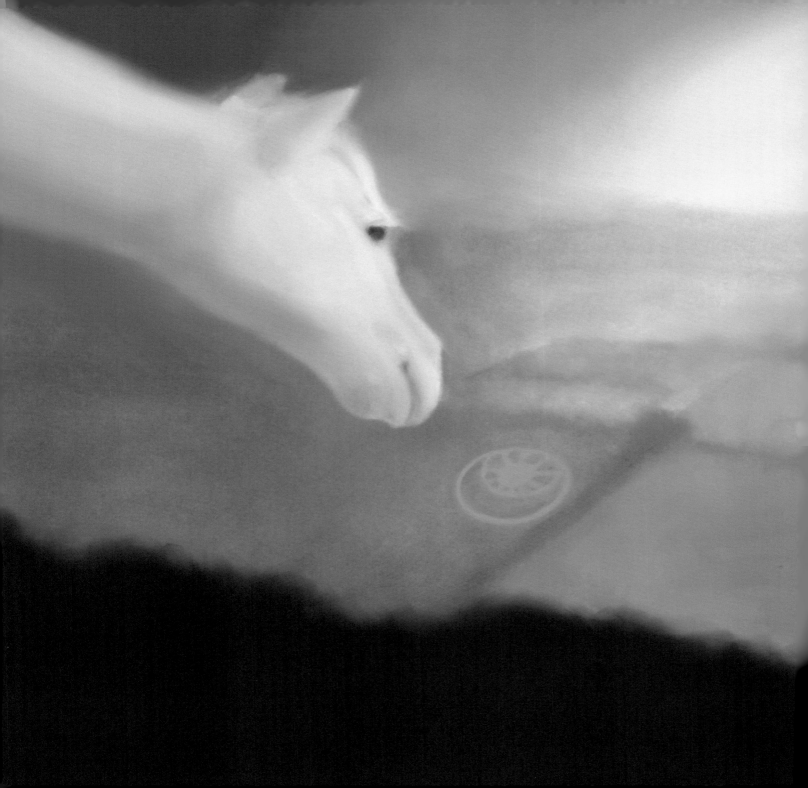

Harry turned around and saw huge circles and fishes and jewels. all carved out of the corn in the cornfields.

"And do you know what happened when I smiled?" asked Will.

Harry had no idea. "What?" he asked.
"People came and wanted to ride me. Long lines of people, all the way to the top of the hill."

Harry thought about this for a long time.
Then he looked at the wonderful designs in the cornfields. A big smile grew all over his face. He felt warm and happy inside.

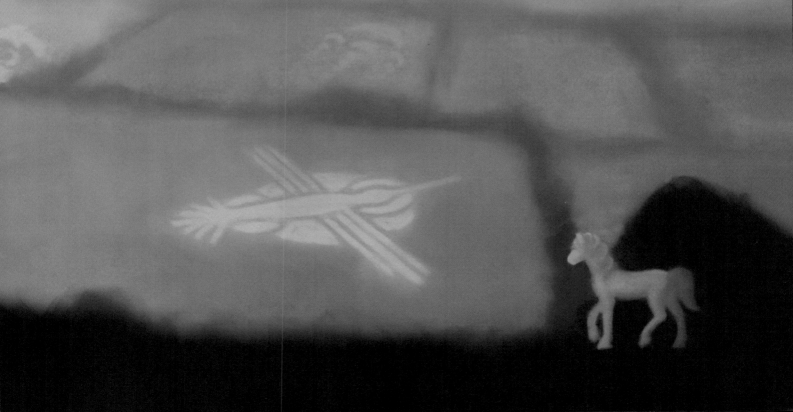

Will saw this and said, "Now the children will want to ride you. They will feel happy because you are happy."

"Go home now," said Will. "Remember, the children will come if you want them to be happy. Also remember that when you feel grouchy, it will not be for ever. That bad feeling will go away."

Harry said thank you and goodbye to Will. As he dreamed his way home he imagined Will was surrounded by many candles. So many that Will glowed and was as bright as daytime.

The next day, back on the carousel, Harry still felt warm and happy inside. He felt even warmer and happier when he saw a long line of children waiting to ride him.

His friends Blue and Red and Bill were all happy for him and smiled.

Real Life Notes

At one time there was a shiny white horse on the carousel at the Mall in Washington, D.C. He was deliberately left unpainted because children preferred him that way. He may still be there.

The newly re-gilded Gold Horse is the first equestrian statue of Joan of Arc. By French sculptor Emmanuel Frémiet, he was first erected in the Place des Pyramides, Paris, in 1874. He now stands facing the Philadelphia Museum of Art in Philadelphia, PA.

When Isaac was three years old, he rode his rocking horse many times a day. He lives in Philadelphia and is still crazy about horses.

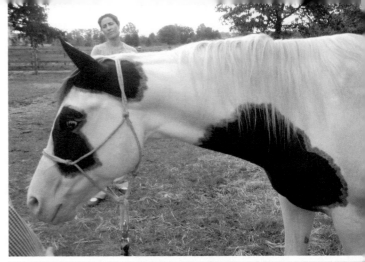

Violet Skye is an equine therapy horse in training at the Cowgirl's Reiki Ranch and Therapeutic Center located in Douglassville, PA. She is a Medicine Hat horse, believed by American Indians to have magical powers.

There are many white horses carved out of chalk on English hillsides; one dates back 3,000 years. Will, the Alton Barnes white horse in Wiltshire, is two hundred years old. On the night of the winter solstice, he is lit by candlelight.

Crop circles appear every year in ever more complex and mysterious designs. Will looks down on the most active area for crop circles in the world. Established in 1995, the Wiltshire Crop Circle Study Group studies the crop circle phenomenon in all its aspects.

CPSIA information can be obtained
at www.ICGtesting.com
Printed in the USA
LVIW010411080512
280796LV00001B